DISCARD

The Legend of
Ponciano Gutiérrez
and the Mountain Thieves

**Pasó por Aquí Series
on the Nuevomexicano
Literary Heritage**

EDITED BY

Genaro M. Padilla,

Enrique R. Lamadrid,

and A. Gabriel Meléndez

To Wolf Croix Cisney,

and Scarlett Ann Underhill,

my grandchildren.

May the love and lore of New Mexico

live in your hearts, as it does in mine.

—A. C.

THE LEGEND OF

Ponciano Gutiérrez

AND THE
Mountain Thieves

THE TELLING BY Casimiro Paiz Jr. (el padre)

INTRODUCTION BY Casey Paiz III (el nieto)

TRANSCRIBED BY Martina Paiz (la nuera)

TRANSLATED BY A. Gabriel Meléndez (el cuñado)

ILLUSTRATIONS BY Amy Córdova

UNIVERSITY OF NEW MEXICO PRESS

Albuquerque

Text © 2013 by the University of New Mexico Press

Illustrations © 2013 by Amy Córdova

All rights reserved. Published 2013

Printed in China

18 17 16 15 14 13   1 2 3 4 5 6

Library of Congress Cataloging-in-Publication Data

Paiz, Casimiro.

The legend of Ponciano Gutiérrez and the mountain thieves / by Casimiro Paiz Jr.; introduction by Casey Paiz III;

transcribed by Martina Paiz; translated by A. Gabriel Meléndez; illustrations by Amy Córdova.

pages cm — (Pasó por aquí series on Nuevomexicano literary heritage)

ISBN 978-0-8263-5239-2 (pbk. : alk. paper) — ISBN 978-0-8263-5240-8 (electronic)

[1. Folklore—New Mexico. 2. Spanish language materials—Bilingual.]

I. Meléndez, A. Gabriel (Anthony Gabriel) II. Córdova, Amy, illustrator. III. Title.

PZ74.1.P35 2013

398.209789—dc23

2012032664

Book design and type composition by Catherine Leonardo

Composed in Adobe Garamond Pro. Display type is Zephyr Regular

R0440718956

CONTENTS

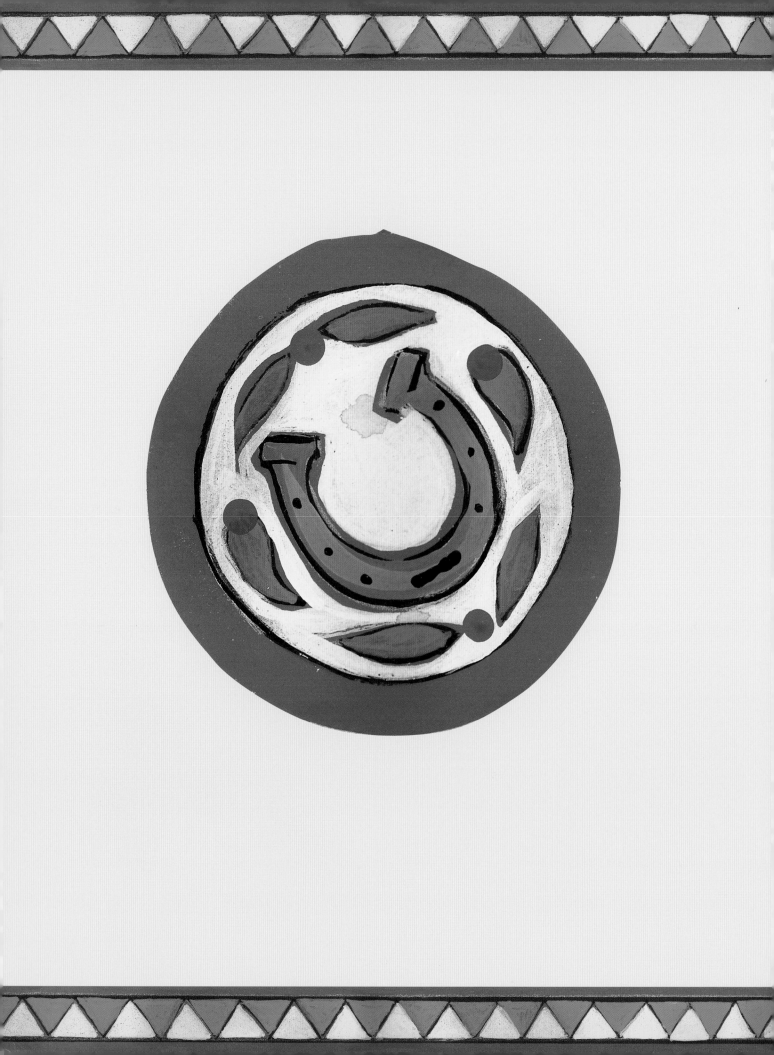

Pasó por Aquí Series Note

THE NUEVOMEXICANO STORYTELLING tradition is varied and delightful. The countless tales and anecdotes mark a wide pathway back to a people's storehouse of knowledge. Retelling any one of these stories takes us from the first spark of its invention to renditions that are meant for our own ears, in our own time. In his compendium titled *Cuento españoles de Colorado y Nuevo México* (*Spanish Folk Tales from Colorado and New Mexico*), Juan Bautista Rael (1900–1993), the foremost collector of Hispano New Mexican folktales, discovered that stories developed in Spain or Mexico were planted into New Mexican communities at the very moment colonists set down roots in the upper Río Grande basin. In the time before television and mass media made their way to the Southwest, people loved to hear stories, and they participated in storytelling sessions that lasted for hours. The primary goal of these storytelling sessions was to entertain listeners. Today we also have come to appreciate that stories made it possible for the group to survive, since in their telling was the accumulated wisdom of the people. They recited things known from the past and retold the narrations as lessons and warnings for future generations.

The Legend of Ponciano Gutiérrez and the Mountain Thieves comes to us along a pathway maintained with special care by one particular family with roots in the Mora Valley. The chain of telling and retelling, by the standards of this tradition, is not excessively long. Since the story involves Ponciano's run-in with Vicente Silva and his bandits, we are safe in saying that the earliest renditions of the tale go back no further than the 1890s. The historical record confirms that Silva and his gang had made Las Vegas, New Mexico, the headquarters of their operations. The gang's decade-long rampage included murders, thefts, illegal land acquisitions, and cattle rustling and lasted for most of the 1880s. By the middle of the next decade, the surviving members were behind bars. Vicente Silva himself died at the hands of his henchmen. Having been ever-willing accomplices, Silva's closest associates reasoned that when Silva killed his own wife, he had "gone too far"—even by the standards of thugs and murderers.

As the Silva crimes diminished, a wave of stories recalling the gang's violent reign and sudden demise swelled. Writer and lawyer Eusebio Chacón colored his 1890 novelette *El hijo de la tormenta* (*Son of the Storm*) with clear allusions to the terror wrought by the Silva gang. In 1896 the territorial prosecutor and journalist Manuel C. de Baca published his account of Silva's crimes, titled "Vicente Silva y sus 40 bandidos," in the newspaper *El sol de mayo*, which he founded in Las Vegas, New Mexico, in 1891. In addition to founding the newspaper, C. de Baca also served as city prosecutor for the town of Las Vegas, which made him the most prominent enemy of Silva's gang, and he came to know a number of its members as each in turn faced him in the courtroom. (For more on the careers of Chacón and C. de Baca, see my book

Spanish-Language Newspapers in New Mexico, 1836–1958).

While men of letters like Eusebio Chacón (1871–1949) and Manuel C. de Baca (1853–1915) were trying to turn the Vicente Silva story into literary and historical texts, Nuevomexicano ranch families and an emerging class of wage-earning railroad workers were busy telling and retelling the story as part of their evolving oral tradition. As a boy growing up in Mora, New Mexico, I recall hearing slivers of the Silva narrative from various older residents. In particular, I recall how on several occasions don Benigno Casados, a veteran of World War I, treated me to the story of how one gang member, Patas de Rana, had come back from prison to take revenge on John Dougherty, the sheriff of Mora County, for the role he had played in getting Patas sent to prison. Don Benigno's story never failed to rivet my

attention, filled as it was with mystery, violence, and retribution. Accounts are consistent in noting that Patas de Rana was a ruthless and despicable character. Don Benigno would tell how Patas de Rana snuck up to the Dougherty place in the dark of night. His movements were those of a stealthy, swift, and deadly *asesino*. John Dougherty lived in the swampy part of town that people called "La China," a neighborhood near the parish church made up of unusually low adobe houses whose walkways were nothing more than waterlogged planks and boards strewn about like stepping-stones for residents to get across the patios. It was pitch dark. Patas de Rana walked up to the thick walls of the Dougherty house. In the light of the kerosene lamp appeared the silhouette of the sheriff in the kitchen window. While the sheriff sat taking his dinner, Patas de Rana, a coward, drew his pistol and without warning aimed and fired into the house, leaving Dougherty to bleed to death. But what always made the hair on my neck stand up was when don Begnino ended the tale by saying, "años después conocí al Patas de Rana cuando trabajábamos en la sesión [years later I met Patas de Rana when we were working on a section gang for the railroad]." According to don Benigno, Patas de Rana was old by then but didn't seem to mind taking credit for the murder of the sheriff.

The gentle, uplifting *Legend of Ponciano Gutiérrez and the Mountain Thieves* was confected somewhere near the time of the crime wave and was told to strengthen the minds and spirits of the young and the brave of heart. It's not clear how widespread its telling became among Nuevomexicanos, but we can be sure that its telling was never absent in the Paiz household in the Mora Valley. Casimiro Paiz Jr., el padre, the raconteur for this book, had the story told to him in the early 1950s by his father Casimiro Paiz Sr., el abuelo, a legend in his own right. Casimiro, el abuelo, was a well-known and respected member of the Mora community. Esteemed by his neighbors, Casimiro, el abuelo, served for twelve years as Mora County sheriff, splitting his tenure as a lawman before and after World War II, in which he honorably served. Returning to Mora in 1945, he went on to attend an FBI training school in El Paso, Texas, while serving his second term as sheriff. Casimiro, el padre, often told the story of Ponciano to his kids, Pamela, Sandra, and Casey, who now live in Denver, Colorado. As Casey Paiz III, el nieto, notes in the introduction, he now delights in sharing the story with his two preschoolers, Thalia and Lucía. The story seeds *querencia*, a deep love and respect for the family's lands in the Mora Valley. Casey's wife, Martina, la nuera, after hearing renditions of the story by both el padre and el nieto, had the presence of mind to transcribe it for this book. I, an in-law always welcomed at the Paiz family home in Mora, have heard this wonderful story and countless others roll off the lips of Casimiro, el padre, a time or two.

In the best tradition of Nuevomexicano lore, this book is the result of all who have been brought together by the gracious act of a good mountain storytelling session.

Storytellers and those who listen to them—transcribers, neighbors, children and grandchildren, visitors and in-laws—all may be taken up in the life that the story breathes back into community. We recognize that in turning this story into a children's book, we are engaging in a new form of storytelling, one that is especially appealing because it affords us a way to invite others to enjoy and delight in the art of this tradition.

As a general editor for the Pasó por Aquí Series, I am most pleased to share the *The Legend of Ponciano Gutiérrez and the Mountain Thieves* with others by adding it to our "*pasitos por aquí*" emerging list of books for children and young readers.

For the *Paso por Aquí* editors,
A. Gabriel Meléndez

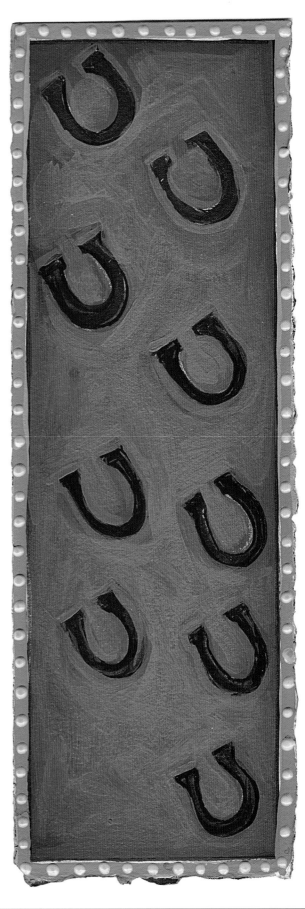

Introduction

Casey Paiz III, el nieto

A TALE THAT HAS BEEN RETOLD for generations in the Paiz family, *The Legend of Ponciano Gutiérrez and the Mountain Thieves* was a favorite bedtime story throughout my childhood, yet it became quiet in my memory until the birth of my first child, Thalia. After I recalled the name Ponciano, the curtains seemed to part, and in my mind's eye I saw Ponciano setting off from my grandmother's house in Mora, New Mexico. Now I wonder if my daughter pictures Ponciano riding on horseback from her Grandfather Casimiro's house across the valley. After dinner one night, we were walking on a dirt road that curves past the property, and Thalia tracked prints, greatly certain that they were made by Ponciano's horse. My wife, who is not from New Mexico but loves it as her own, insisted that we write down the story of Ponciano, lest this treasure be lost.

Introducción

Casey Paiz III, el nieto

SE HA CONTADO UNA LEYENDA EN LA familia de los Paiz tras las generaciones con tanta frecuencia que *La leyenda de Ponciano Gutiérrez y los ladrones de la sierra* se había convertido en un cuento de cuna a lo largo de mi niñez, y sin embargo se había dormido en mi memoria hasta el nacimiento de mi primera niña, Thalia. Cuando se me vino a la cabeza el nombre "Ponciano," las cortinas del tiempo se abrieron, y vi a Ponciano agarrando camino, dejando atrás la casa de mi abuela en Mora, Nuevo México. Ahora me pongo a pensar si mi hija ve a Ponciano montado a caballo alejándose de la casa de su Abuelo Casimiro por el valle. Una tarde después de la cena caminábamos por un camino de tierra que pasa a un lado de la casa de los Paiz, y Thalia comenzó a rastrear una huellas que con gran certeza anunció que las había hecho el caballo de Ponciano Gutiérrez. Mi esposa, que no es nativa de Nuevo México pero que ama está tierra como si lo fuera, insistió que escribiéramos el cuento de Ponciano a no ser que este tesoro se perdiese.

The Legend of Ponciano Gutiérrez and the Mountain Thieves

Once upon a time, in the Mora Valley of New Mexico, there lived a farmer named Ponciano Gutiérrez. Ponciano awoke early one spring morning to do some chores on his *ranchito*. The first thing he needed to do that day was mend a fence that had been broken by the heavy winter snow. As Ponciano was mending the fence, he started to think about the other things he needed to do to prepare for his spring planting. He needed to go to the bank in Santa Fe to withdraw some money from his savings and buy more seed at the general store. Now Ponciano knew that taking the main road to Santa Fe was a long trip: seven days by horse to get there, seven days to return. This would keep him away from his ranch for two weeks, and Ponciano didn't like the idea of being away from his ranch for two whole weeks.

La leyenda de Ponciano Gutiérrez y los ladrones de la sierra

Una vez en el Valle de Mora Nuevo México, vivía un ranchero llamado Ponciano Gutiérrez. Ponciano se despertó de mañana un día de primavera para hacer unos quehaceres en su ranchito. Lo primero que tenía en mente hacer ese día era componer un cerco que las nevadas pesadas del invierno pasado habían tumbado. Conforme iba componiendo el cerco, comenzó a pensar de las demás cosas que tenía que hacer para prepararse para barbechar esa primavera. Tenía que ir al banco en Santa Fe a sacar un dinero de su cuenta de ahorros para comprar semilla en el comercio. Bien, Ponciano sabía que tomar el camino principal a Santa Fe sería una larga jornada: siete días a caballo para llegar y siete días para regresar. Esto le causaría estar fuera de su ranchito por una quincena, y a Ponciano no le apetecía la idea de estar lejos de su rancho por dos semanas completas.

17

Fortunately he knew of another route to Santa Fe: crossing the Pecos Wilderness high in the Sangre de Cristo Mountains. It was only two days' journey, and this sounded like a much better idea to Ponciano. Though it was a much more difficult and dangerous route, Ponciano knew the mountains very well, and he had a strong and agile horse. So after careful consideration, he decided he would make the trip through the Pecos Wilderness to Santa Fe.

Por ventura él conocía otra ruta a Santa Fe: cruzaría las montañas enormes de la Sangre de Cristo pasando por la zona del Pecos, la región virgen de la floresta. Esto sólo le costaría dos días de viaje, y esto le pareció una mejor idea a Ponciano. Aunque sería una ruta mucho más peligrosa y difícil, Ponciano tenía gran conocimiento de la sierra y su caballo era ágil y poderoso. Así que después de pensarlo bien decidió hacer el viaje por la región virgen de la floresta de Pecos para llegar a Santa Fe.

The next morning Ponciano woke up extra early, before daybreak, to prepare for his journey. He put an extra blanket on his horse and packed an extra jacket, a rifle, his pistol, and some provisions, including *carne seca*, *manzana seca*, nuts, and a canteen of water. With these provisions ready, Ponciano led his horse from the barn, and he put on his hat and started riding toward the Pecos Wilderness trailhead.

El día siguiente Ponciano madrugó, levantándose antes que rayara el sol, para alistarse para el viaje. Puso una manta gorda en su caballo y empacó su mejor chamarra, su rifle, su pistola y algunas proviciones como carne seca, manzana seca, nueces y una cantina de agua. Listo con estas proviciones, Ponciano cabrestró su caballo, sacándolo de la caballeriza, y se puso su sombrero y se dirigió a la puerta de entrada de la vereda que daba a la zona virgen del Pecos.

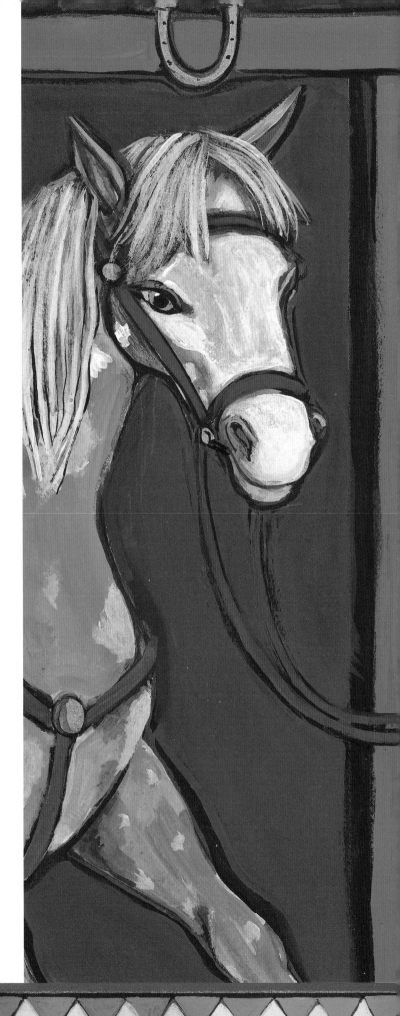

Once on the trail, Ponciano noticed he was not the only horse rider in the Pecos Wilderness. In fact, there were more tracks in the snow than he expected to see, considering it was very early in the spring, and most people did not go far into the wilderness until summertime. By midmorning Ponciano was deep into the wilderness, and he had counted the tracks in the snow: there were six riders, and they were not far away from him.

An hour later, Ponciano rode through El Cañón del Miedo—Fear Canyon—and entered a clearing. Suddenly he was upon the riders, and he knew exactly who they were. It was none other than Vicente Silva and his gang of bank robbers! This notorious group had mercilessly terrorized the people of New Mexico and evaded the law for months.

They surrounded and overpowered Ponciano immediately. Not wanting to be discovered in their mountain hideout, they discussed what to do with the intruder. One of the bandits suggested they tie him up and leave him for dead. Another suggested they take him as a hostage. Still another suggested the unspeakable: he said they should kill him. Ponciano, being a quick-witted man, interrupted them with a story of his own criminal exploits. He told them of the crimes he had committed and of his many polished criminal skills, such as pickpocketing, sharpshooting, and knot tying. At first they were unimpressed, but Ponciano challenged their best pickpocket to a contest.

Una vez en la vereda, Ponciano se dio cuenta que no era el único jinete en la floresta de Pecos. Había muchas más huellas en la nieve de las que esperaba ver en vista de que aún era temprano en la primavera, y la mayor parte de la gente no profundizaba en la floresta hasta el verano. Para antes de mediodía Ponciano estaba ya en plena zona virgen, y ya había calculado el número de huellas en la nieve: eran seis hombres a caballo, y no estaban muy lejos de él.

Después de una hora, Ponciano cabalgaba por el Cañón del Miedo y salió a una llanura. De repente se enfrentó con los hombres a caballo e inmediatamente los reconoció. ¡Era Vicente Silva y su gavilla de ladrones! Estos infames malhechores habían asaltado a bancos y aterrorizado a la gente de Nuevo México y evadido la ley por meses.

Pronto rodearon y dominaron a Ponciano. Por nada del mundo querían que se descubriera su escondite en la sierra y empezaron a discutir qué hacer con el intruso. Uno de los bandidos propuso que lo ataran con cabresto y dejarlo por muerto. Otro sugerió que lo llevaran de rehén. Y otro más pronunció lo inpensable: dijo que lo mataran. Como Ponciano era un hombre listo, los interrumpió con un largo relato de sus propios hechos criminales. En detalle les contó de los crímenes que había cometido y de sus destrezas como bandido, tales como su talento como ratero, tirador experto y maestro en el arte de atar nudos. En un principio no le hicieron caso hasta que Ponciano los desafió a una contienda de rateros.

"Who is the best pickpocket in your gang?" asked Ponciano.

Patas de Rana stepped forward and said, "I am the quickest pickpocket around."

Pointing his finger across the brush, Ponciano said, "Do you see that lone pine tree with the eagle's nest?"

"Yes," replied Patas de Rana.

"In that nest there are eggs," said Ponciano. "And if you can steal them, without disturbing the mama eagle, you will indeed prove that you are a masterful pickpocket. But if the mother eagle spies you, she will claw your eyes out with her sharp talons." Ponciano raised his finger. "To prove I am an equally talented pickpocket, I will take those eggs and return them to her nest without her noticing."

Patas de Rana accepted the challenge and crept through the dense underbrush.

He was almost to the pine tree when Ponciano told Silva to untie him so that he could play a little trick on Patas de Rana. He said, "Untie me, so I can show you all how crafty I can be! Anyway, since you have my gun and my horse, and all your men are watching me, you know I can't escape."

Silva was intrigued and agreed to his request, and Ponciano set out through the underbrush to the pine tree.

—¿Quién es el mejor carterista entre ustedes?—preguntó Ponciano.

El Patas de Rana se puso en primera fila y dijo—, ¡Yo soy el más liviano carterista de la gavilla!

Fue entonces que Ponciano señaló sobre el ramaje y dijo—, ¿Ves aquel pinabete solitario en el que está un nido de águila?

—Sí—respondió el Patas de Rana.

—En aquel nido hay unos huevos—dijo Ponciano—. Y si puedes robarlos, sin que te sienta el águila, entonces sí mostrarás que eres un maestro entre rateros. Sin embargo si te espía el águila mamá te sacará los ojos de la cara con sus garras filudas—. Ponciano alzó un dedo—, Pero para probar que yo estoy al tanto de ti como carterista, tomaré eso mismos huevos y los pondré en el nido de nuevo sin que la mamá se dé cuenta.

Patas de Rana aceptó el desafío y se metió al espeso ramaje.

Estaba por llegar al pino cuando Ponciano hizo que Silva lo desatara para jugarle una trampa a Patas de Rana. Dijo—¡Desátame para enseñarte qué tan sagaz puedo ser! En todo caso tú tienes mi pistola y mi caballo, y todos tus hombres me están vigilando y ya sabes que no puedo escaparme.

Silvia era curioso y consintió, y Ponciano se deslizó por entre el ramaje hasta llegar al pino.

Being much faster and more agile than Patas de Rana, Ponciano easily caught up with him as both men quietly climbed the tall pine. When Patas de Rana reached the nest, Ponciano slowly and quietly reached one hand up into the nest and under the eagle's feathers. He felt for the first egg. Then he carefully removed it and slipped it into his coat pocket. As Patas de Rana went for the second egg, Ponciano reached into the thief's pocket and relieved him of his first treasure. And in this manner, all the eggs in the nest were transferred from raptor to thief to farmer.

Pero como Ponciano era mucho más diestro y veloz que Patas de Rana, fácilmente lo alcanzó y a la par que los dos trepaban el alto árbol. Cuando Patas de Rana llegó al nido, despacio y sigilosamente metió una mano en el nido debajo de las plumas del águila. Pulsó por un primer huevo. Luego lo sacó con cuidado y lo puso en el bolsillo de su chamarra. Mientras Patas de Rana fue sacando el segundo huevo, Ponciano metió la mano en el bolsillo del ladrón y le quitó su primera joya. Y en esta forma todos los huevos del nido se trasladaron del ave raptora al ladrón y luego al ranchero.

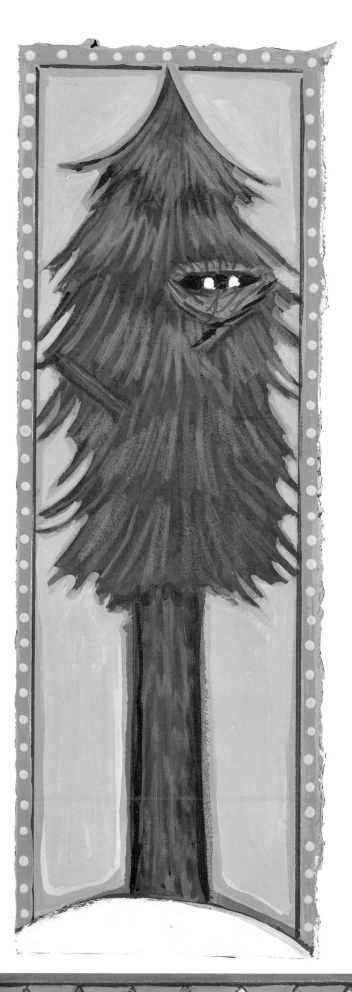

Using his skill, Ponciano quickly descended the tree and returned to the gang before the thief knew what had happened.

When Patas de Rana returned to the group, he confidently said to Silva, "*¡Mira!* I have stolen the eggs from underneath the eagle's feathers!" He reached into his pocket to withdraw the goods, and his eyes grew big with bewilderment: his pockets were completely empty! Bumbling around, he said, "But the eggs! They were just here!"

Usando su astucia, Ponciano pronto se bajó del árbol y volvió a la gavilla antes de que el ladrón supiera qué había pasado.

Cuando Patas de Rana se presentó ante la gavilla, muy engreído le dijo a Silva— ¡Mira! ¡He robado los huevos de entre las garras del águila!—Metió la mano al bolsillo para sacar las joyas, y sus ojos se abrieron con el susto: ¡su bolsillo estaba completamente vacío! Balbuceó—, ¡Pero los huevos! ¡Aquí estaban!

Ponciano extended his hand with the eggs and asked, "Are these the eggs you are looking for?"

At this the gang exploded in laughter at the befuddled thief's expense.

Keeping up his end of the deal, Ponciano returned the eggs to the great raptor's nest. Impressed with Ponciano's thieving skills, the bandits allowed him another contest.

Ponciano asked, "Who is the best sharpshooter in the gang?"

El Tusa stepped forward and boasted, "I am the quickest draw in all of Mora County and the deadliest in the valley!"

Ponciano pulled one silver coin from his pocket and challenged El Tusa to shoot it in midair. The buck-toothed assassin accepted, and Ponciano tossed the coin up. El Tusa drew his pistol and fired three shots, hitting the coin once before it fell to the ground. The gang cheered in approval at El Tusa's skill. Then Ponciano asked him if he could hit six coins before they hit the ground. The sharpshooter declared it was an impossible feat that no man could do.

Ponciano replied, "Give me a pistol and let me show you." Then he instructed El Tusa to throw six coins into the air. Ponciano aimed his pistol and fired six rounds, hitting each of the coins before they hit the earth. The gang cheered for they had never seen anyone shoot so well before.

Ponciano extendió la mano con los huevos y le preguntó—¿Son estos, los huevos que buscas?

Con esto los socios se descosieron en carcajadas a costo del ladrón confundido.

Como había cumplido con su promesa, Ponciano devolvió los huevos al nido del ave raptora. Asombrados con las artimañas de Ponciano, los bandidos le permitieron otro desafío.

Ponciano les preguntó—¿Quién es el mejor tirador de ustedes?

El Tusa se paró y parándose el cuello declaró—¡Yo soy el mejor y más rápido tirador de bala en todo el Condado de Mora y por cierto el más cierto en el valle!

Ponciano sacó una moneda de plata de su bolsillo y desafió al Tusa que le pegara con un tiro en el aire. El asesino de dientes salidos aceptó, y Ponciano lanzó la moneda al aire. El Tusa desenvainó su pistola y disparó tres tiros, pegándole a la moneda una vez antes que diera en el suelo. La gavilla aplaudía como locos la destreza del Tusa. Entonces Ponciano le preguntó si podía darle a seis monedas antes que cayeran en la tierra. El tirador declaró que esto era imposible y que ningún hombre podía hacer tal cosa.

Ponciano contestó—Tráiganme una pistola y yo le enseñaré que sí se puede—. Entonces mandó que el Tusa tirara seis monedas al aire. Ponciano apuntó su pistola y disparó seis veces, dándole un tiro a cada una de las monedas antes de que dieran con la tierra. La gavilla aplaudió pues nunca habían visto otro que pudiera tirar en tal forma.

With this, Silva and his bandits invited Ponciano to join their gang. Ponciano accepted their offer and insisted he show them one more trick.

"I need your longest and strongest length of rope," he said.

The bandits eagerly produced one for their new friend. With instant authority, Ponciano commanded the first man to extend both of his hands. In a flash, Ponciano looped the rope securely around the man's wrist so tightly that he could scarcely move. Ponciano pointed to the next man and instructed him to extend his arms also. In this fashion, Ponciano applied the same knot to all six outlaws, who were mesmerized by his skills. The gang agreed that these were the fastest and tightest knots they had ever seen, and they would have clapped had their hands not been bound.

Ponciano had one more surprise in store for the gang. "You know what?" he said. "Now that you all have these pretty bows on your wrists, you're ready to meet the sheriff of Santa Fe."

Una vez hecho esto, Silva y sus ladrones invitaron a Ponciano a juntarse a la gavilla. Ponciano aceptó pero insistió que lo dejaran mostrar un truco más.

—Necesito el más largo y más fuerte cabresto—dijo.

La gavilla lo produjo con mucho entusiasmo. Con plena autoridad, Ponciano ordenó que el primer hombre extendiera los brazos. En tanto que nada, Ponciano tiró un lazo sobre los brazos del ladrón y lo estiro tan fuerte que aquel hombre ya no se pudo desatar. Ponciano le señaló al segundo ladrón que hiciera lo mismo. De esta forma, Ponciano les hizo el mismo nudo a los seis ladrones que aún estaban embelesados con su arte. Los de la gavilla se pusieron de acuerdo en que estos eran los más rápidos y más seguros nudos que jamás habían visto, y lo hubieran aplaudido si tan solo tuvieran sus manos libres.

Ponciano tenía una sorpresa más preparada para la gavilla.—¿Saben qué señores?—les dijo—ahora con estos moños que traen en las muñecas están relistos para hacerle una visita al alguacil mayor de Santa Fe.

The bandits began to struggle, but Ponciano looped the long end of the rope around his saddle horn and with a stern "YAW!" commanded his trusty horse to start the chain gang down the mountain through the Santa Barbara Forest toward Santa Fe.

When they arrived at the capital, the sheriff praised Ponciano to the high heavens for single-handedly doing what all of Santa Fe's law enforcement was not able to do for months: capture Silva and his band of thieves. As he took custody of the outlaws, the sheriff promised to lock them up and throw away the key. The people of Santa Fe were so grateful, they presented Ponciano with a generous reward, which Ponciano was able to use to buy seed for his farm and put what was left over into his savings, instead of withdrawing money from his account at the Bank of Santa Fe.

Los ladrones empezaron a inquietarse, pero Ponciano había enredado lo que quedaba del cabresto en la bola de su silla y soltando un estridente "¡AJÚAH!" hizo que su caballo leal diera inicio a la cadena de reos para bajar la montaña por el tupido monte de Santa Bárbara camino hacia Santa Fe.

Cuando llegaron a la capital, el alguacil mayor halagó sin tregua a Ponciano por haber hecho solo lo que todas las autoridades de Santa Fe no pudieron lograr en meses: capturar a Silva y su gavilla de ladrones. Tomando cargo de los malhechores, el alguacil mayor prometió encarcelarlos y aventar las llaves lejos de sus celdas. Los ciudadanos de Santa Fe estaban tan agradecidos que le dieron una recompensa lo suficiente grande para permitir que Ponciano comprara semilla para sus cultivos y para añadir a su cuenta de ahorros en el Banco de Santa Fe.

The next day Ponciano started his journey back over the mountains to his ranchito. His two little girls were waiting for him. They were excited to see him because they couldn't wait to show him the new baby *pollitos*. That spring, Ponciano plowed and planted his fields and grew more fruits and vegetables than any other farmer in the Mora Valley has, before or since.

El día siguiente Ponciano comenzó su viaje a través de la sierra que lo llevaría de nuevo a su ranchito. Cuando llegó sus dos hijitas lo esperaban. Ellas estaban ansiosas de enseñarle los pollitos recién nacidos. Esa primavera, Ponciano barbechó y sembró sus campos y cosechó más fruta y verduras que cualquier otro granjero en el Valle de Mora, un logro sin rival que no se vio ni antes, ni después.

THE END

FIN